WHO LOVES THE FALL?

by **Bob Raczka**

illustrated by

Judy Stead

Your AV² Media Enhanced book gives you a fiction readalong online. Log on to www.av2books.com and enter the unique book code from this page to use your readalong.

AV² Readalong Navigation

Go to **www.av2books.com**, and enter this book's unique code.

BOOK CODE

N878559

AV² by Weigl brings you media enhanced books that support active learning.

First Published by

ALBERT WHITMAN & COMPANY
Publishing children's books since 1919

HIGHLIGHTED TEXT

HOME

CLOSE

START READING

READ

TITLE INFORMATION

INFO

PAGE TURNING

BACK NEXT

PAGE PREVIEW

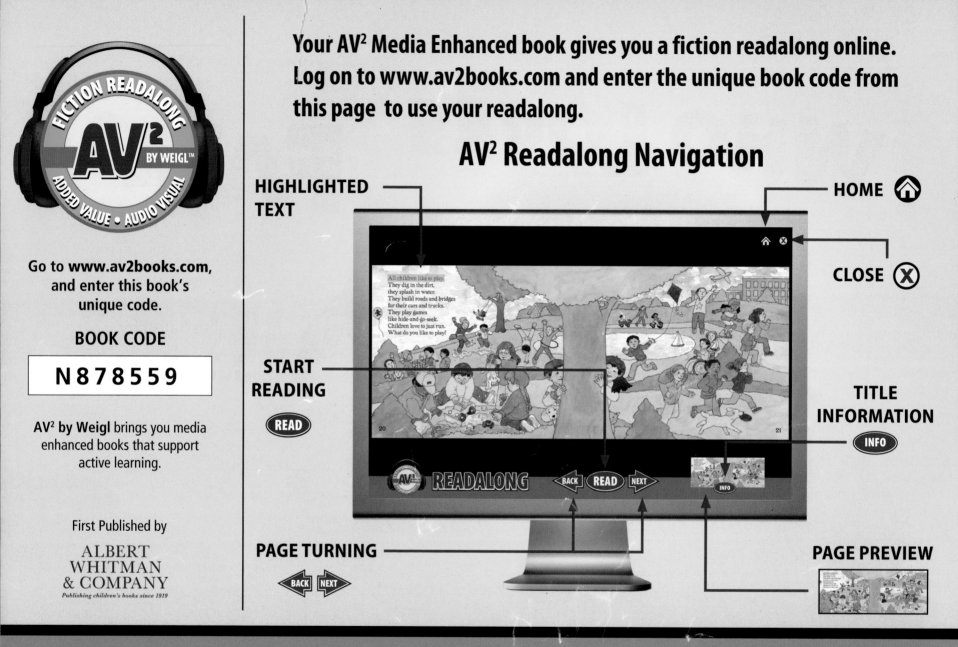

Published by AV² by Weigl
350 5th Avenue, 59th Floor New York, NY 10118
Website: www.av2books.com   www.weigl.com

Printed in the United States of America in North Mankato, Minnesota
1 2 3 4 5 6 7 8 9 0 17 16 15 14 13

052013
WEP250413

Library of Congress Control Number: 2013940833

ISBN 978-1-62127-910-5 (hardcover)
ISBN 978-1-48961-497-1 (single-user eBook)
ISBN 978-1-48961-498-8 (multi-user eBook)

Text copyright ©2007 by Bob Raczka.
Illustrations copyright ©2007 by Judy Stead.
Published in 2007 by Albert Whitman & Company.

Who loves the fall?

Rakers,

leapers,

6

corn-crop reapers.

Growers,

pickers,

taffy lickers.

9

Quilters,

choppers,

helicopters.

Winged migrators,

hibernators.

Hooters,

howlers,

loud meowers.

15

Bonfire builders,

pie-crust fillers,

even former caterpillars!

Adders,

School Spelling Bee

spellers,

show-and-tellers.

23

Passers,

punters,

pumpkin hunters.

Trickers,

28

treaters,

turkey eaters.

30

Don't you love the fall?

FALL FACTS

To **reap** means to cut down or harvest a crop, especially tall crops like corn and wheat. In the old days, farmers reaped by hand with curved blades called sickles. Today, they drive big machines with many blades called combines.

A **maple tree** produces seeds that blow free from its branches in the fall. The seeds are shaped like propeller blades. This allows them to spin like helicopters away from the tree, where they have a better chance of growing into new trees.

To **migrate** means to move from one place to another. In the fall, many types of birds migrate from the North to the South, where the winters are warmer. When geese migrate, they fly in large "V" formations and take turns being the leader.

To **hibernate** means to sleep through cold weather. It's how animals like bears survive winter, when food is scarce. In the fall, these animals store up fat in their bodies by eating more. Then they find a den to sleep in and live off the fat until spring.

A **monarch butterfly** starts life as an egg on a milkweed plant. It hatches into a caterpillar, which eats the milkweed leaves. Then it hangs from a twig and transforms into a pupa in a cocoon. Two weeks later, it emerges as a butterfly. In the late summer to early fall, the monarch migrates south.